Dear Parent:

Congratulations! Your child is taking the first steps on an exciting journey. The destination? Independent reading!

STEP INTO READING® will help your child get there. The program offers five steps to reading success. Each step includes fun stories and colorful art. There are also Step into Reading Sticker Books, Step into Reading Math Readers, Step into Reading Phonics Readers, Step into Reading Write-In Readers, and Step into Reading Phonics Boxed Sets—a complete literacy program with something for every child.

Learning to Read, Step by Step!

Ready to Read   Preschool–Kindergarten
• big type and easy words • rhyme and rhythm • picture clues
For children who know the alphabet and are eager to begin reading.

Reading with Help   Preschool–Grade 1
• basic vocabulary • short sentences • simple stories
For children who recognize familiar words and sound out new words with help.

Reading on Your Own   Grades 1–3
• engaging characters • easy-to-follow plots • popular topics
For children who are ready to read on their own.

Reading Paragraphs   Grades 2–3
• challenging vocabulary • short paragraphs • exciting stories
For newly independent readers who read simple sentences with confidence.

Ready for Chapters   Grades 2–4
• chapters • longer paragraphs • full-color art
For children who want to take the plunge into chapter books but still like colorful pictures.

STEP INTO READING® is designed to give every child a successful reading experience. The grade levels are only guides. Children can progress through the steps at their own speed, developing confidence in their reading, no matter what their grade.

Remember, a lifetime love of reading starts with a single step!

W9-BQX-407

Step into Reading, Random House, and the Random House colophon are registered trademarks of Random House, Inc.

Visit us on the Web!
StepIntoReading.com
randomhouse.com/kids

Educators and librarians, for a variety of teaching tools, visit us at RHTeachersLibrarians.com

ISBN: 978-0-7364-3027-2 (trade) — ISBN: 978-0-7364-8122-9 (lib. bdg.)

Printed in the United States of America   10 9 8 7 6 5 4 3 2 1

Disney

ALICE
in
WONDERLAND

Adapted by Pamela Bobowicz

Illustrated by the Disney Storybook Artists

Random House 🏠 New York

Alice was a young girl.

She liked to daydream.

She dreamed

of a strange land.

She wanted to go there.

A white rabbit ran by.
He looked at
his pocket watch.

"I'm late!"

he cried.

Alice ran after him.

The rabbit went
under a tree.

He went down a hole.

Alice followed.

She fell

down, down, down.

Alice was in

a strange forest.

She followed
the rabbit
to his house.

Alice went
into the house.
She ate some cookies.

The cookies made her
grow and grow.
She grew too big
for the house!

A dodo bird
gave her a carrot.
She ate the carrot.
It made her shrink!

Now Alice was smaller
than the bird.
The White Rabbit
ran away.

Alice searched for
the rabbit again.
She met some flowers.
They could talk!
They asked her what
kind of flower she was.

"I'm a girl, not a flower,"
Alice told them.

The flowers laughed.

Alice ran away.

Next Alice met
the Mad Hatter
and the March Hare.

They were having

a tea party.

The Mad Hatter

had a cake.

It was

under his hat!

He let Alice
make a wish.
She wished to find
the White Rabbit.

Alice was tired.

She could not find

the White Rabbit.

No one could help her.

Then Alice met a cat.
"I'm lost,"
she told him.

The cat asked Alice
where she wanted to go.
Alice didn't know.
"Then you're not lost!"
the cat said.

The cat led Alice

to a castle garden.

The White Rabbit
was there!
He worked for
the Queen of Hearts.

Alice wanted
to go home.
She told the Queen.

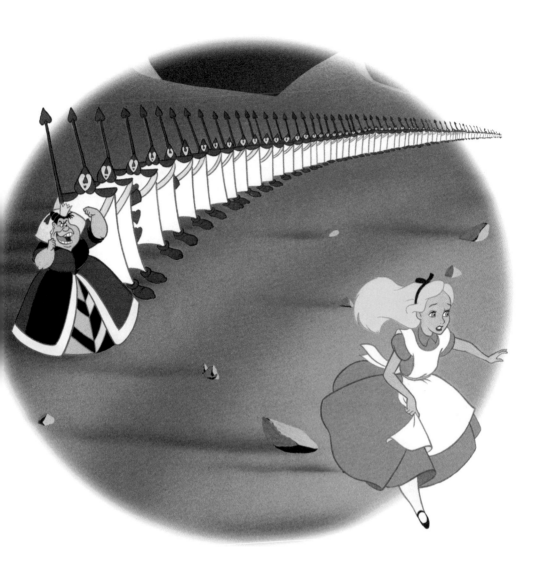

The Queen was angry.

Alice ran away.

Alice heard
her cat purring.
She opened her eyes.
She was home again.
It had all been a dream!